Diego, The Lonely Cat

Written and Illustrated by Jeanne Conway

"It's a perfect day to roam around the neighborhood. What new things will I see?" said Diego.

"I love all my friends in the neighborhood." Diego said with a smile. "But there's one thing that I love more."

"I love my family most of all." Diego said.

"Come here Diego!," said Juan and Maria, "We've got a treat for you."

Everyday Diego visits his friends: the lady across the street, Jacob who lives nearby, the firefighters, the school children, Wilma who delivers the mail, and the librarians.

One day Diego came home and thought "Why are there so many boxes in our house?"

"We're moving tomorrow Diego," said Juan, "to a brand new house!"

The next day Juan and Maria put Diego in a carrying case.

"Oh no, I hate that carrying case!" Diego thought. "I'll find a way to break out of it. I'll get back to our house in time for the move."

Diego! ---- Diego!

When it was time for the Sanchez family to leave, Juan and Maria could not find Diego. Mama said that they must leave but they could come back tomorrow to look for Diego.

Later that day, Diego returned to his house but no one was there.

"They left without me!" he cried. "I'll just wait here for them. They'll come back for me."

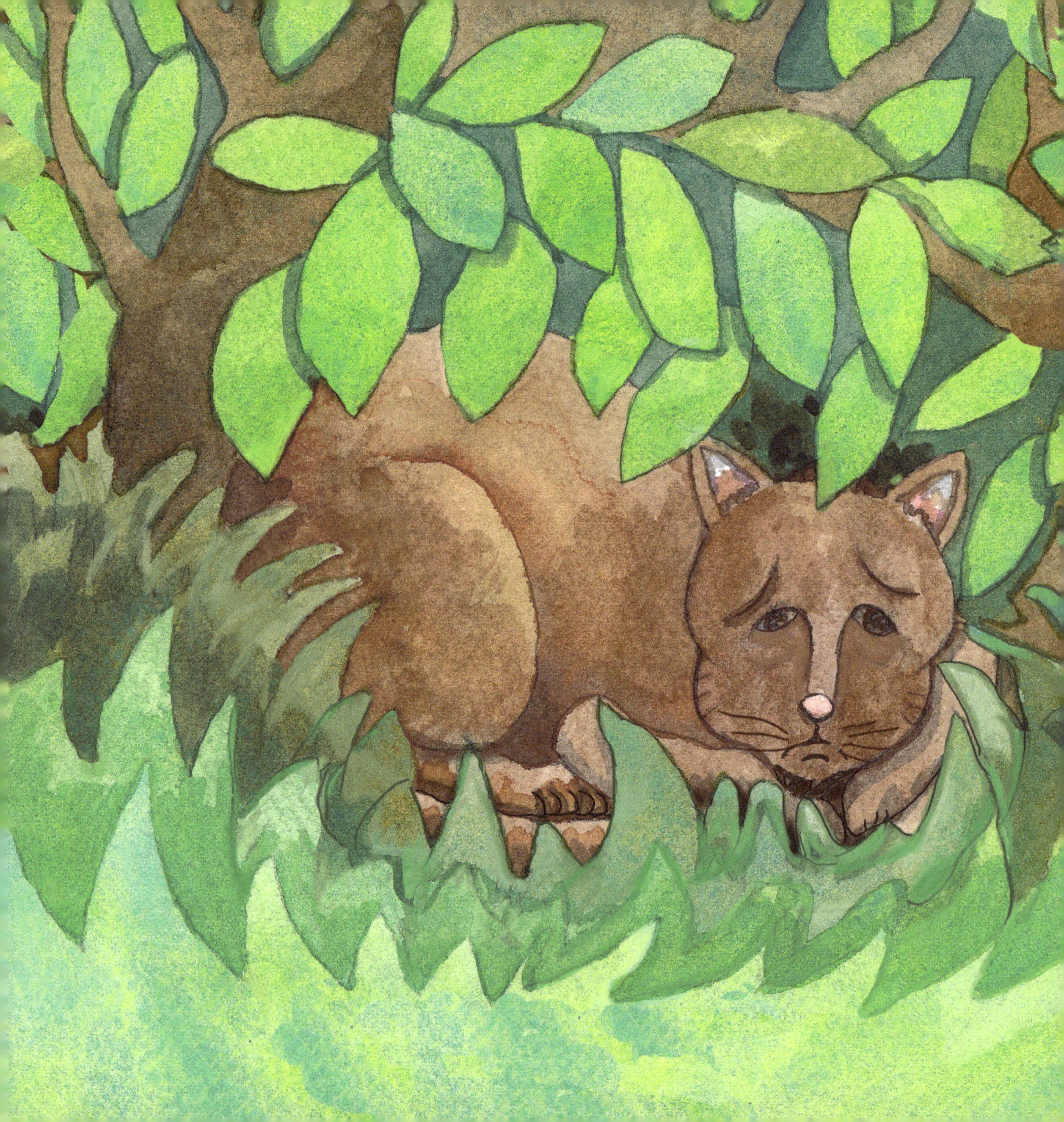

"I guess I can hide under this bush." Diego thought. "Oh, it's getting so dark and I'm cold."

If cats could cry, Diego would. "What will I do? I'm hungry. Who's going to take care of me? Where are Juan and Maria? I am so lonely!"

The next morning, Diego thought "Well, I've just got to take care of myself. I'll find food and maybe someone can give me a place to stay. I can be brave. I will be brave!"

"I'll try the lady across the street. She likes me." thought Diego.

"Here is some food Diego," she said "but I can't let you into my house. I'm allergic to cats."

Maybe Jacob who lives down the street will help Diego. "Come on and play ball with me, Diego."

Diego thought "That would be OK but not for long. Jacob's dog looks mean. I'm scared of him."

-"I'll try the firefighters. They like me and always give me some food." Diego stayed for a while but then the fire alarm sounded. "Oh, that is too scary a sound for me!"

"I know what I'll do! I'll stop by the school playground. One of the children might take me home with them." But that doesn't work.

The teachers shoo him away from the playground.

Diego saw Wilma, the lady who delivers the mail. "I'll bet she will help me!".

"Here's a treat, Diego," Wilma said, "but I can't take you home with me. My landlord doesn't allow pets."

"I'll try the librarians. We are good friends - they will help me." thought Diego.

"Come and join us for story time, Diego." said Mrs. Davis, the head librarian.

"Diego, you can come home with me." said the kind-hearted Mrs. Allen who was Mrs. Davis's assistant.

"Oh thank you Mrs. Allen!" smiled Diego with his best cat smile.

Once Diego arrived at Mrs. Allen's house, he felt sad.

"I want to go home. What if Juan and Maria are there right now looking for me? I'm lonely for them. I will find my way back to our house!"

Diego found his house and thought "I know Juan and Maria will look for me. I will wait for them here."

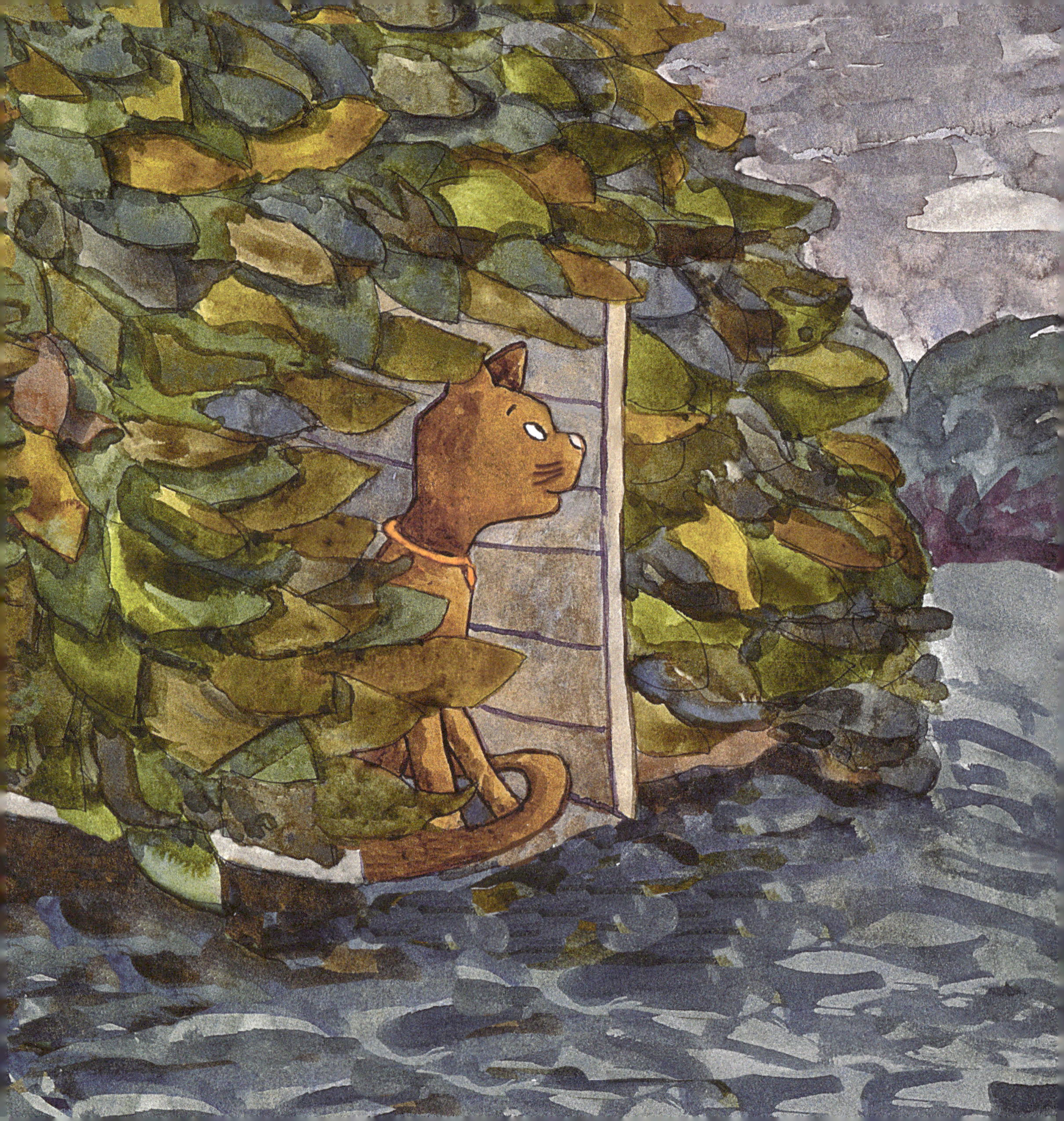

"I'll stay near the house," thought Diego, "There's an old box I can sleep in. It looks like it's going to storm, I hope there isn't any thunder - it's so loud."

In the morning it was still raining but the thunderstorm was over. "I know a safe place where I won't get wet."

Diego thought, "There's a car next door and I can hide underneath it."

"Diego!, Diego!" Diego heard someone call his name. Diego thought "That voice sounds familiar. Could it be?"

Diego could hear footsteps and then saw some shoes. "I know those shoes!" Diego thought.

. . . "Diego, Diego! Where are you?" the voice called again. Diego's ears perked up. "It is Juan!"

Juan came back!

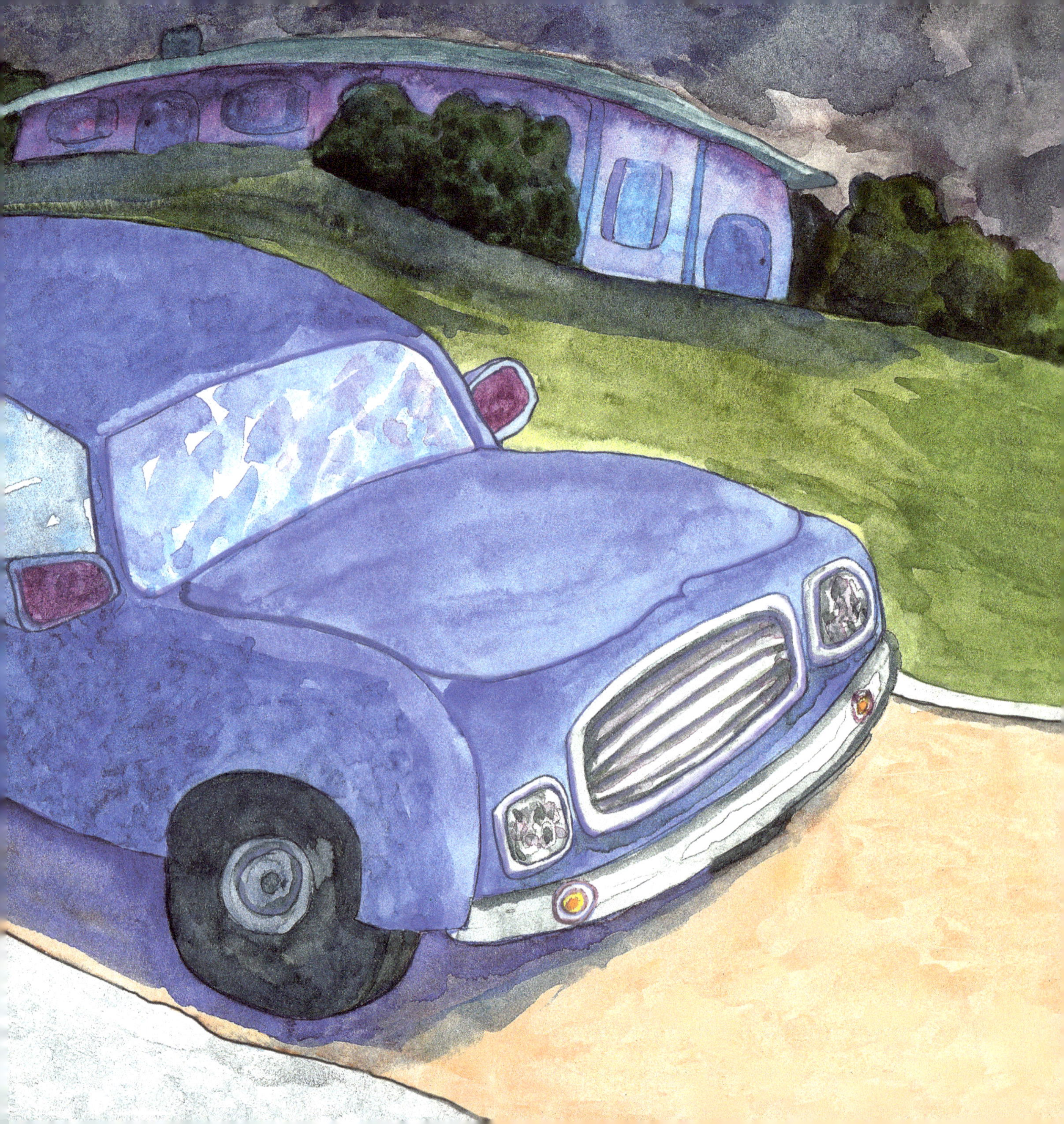

"I've found you at last!," Juan said with a happy smile, "Maria and I have been looking all over for you!"

"Let's go home, Diego!" Juan said.

Diego purred and held on to Juan.

"I'm home!" Diego said as he smiled with his best and widest cat smile. He purred with happiness. "I am not lonely anymore!"

About the Author/Illustrator

Jeanne Conway is an artist, illustrator, children's book writer and art educator from St. Louis, Missouri. She is a member of the Society of Children's Writers and Illustrators. You can view more of her art and her children's books on her website, https://www.jeanniespaintings.com.

For Julie with love and thanks for finding the real Diego.

Diego, The Lonely Cat

Text and Artwork copyright © 2022 by Jeanne Conway

All rights reserved. No part of this book may be reproduced in any form or by any electronic or mechanical means including information storage and retrieval systems – except in the case of brief quotations embodied in critical articles or reviews – without permission in writing from its publisher, Clear Fork Publishing.

Summary: Diego is a friendly and curious cat. He loves to roam and visit people. On the day that his family moves to a new house, Diego cannot be found. Maria and Juan look everywhere for him but no success.

Later, when Diego returns to his now-empty home, his family is gone. What will Diego do? Who will take care of him? "Diego, The Lonely Cat" is the story of how Diego uses his courage and intelligence to find his home and family.

Clear Fork Publishing
P.O. Box 870
102 S. Swenson
Stamford, Texas 79553
(325)773-5550
www.clearforkpublishing.com

Printed and Bound in the
United States of America.
ISBN - 978-1-950169-75-7

An Imprint
of Clear Fork
Publishing